PETER KAVANAGH

Arthur the Outlaw

H O D D E R
Wayland

an imprint of Hodder Children's Books

CHAPTER ONE
Arthur's Idea

Arthur needed an escape plan.

It was a noisy Monday morning in the playground of Knotty Ham School. He'd had all weekend but he hadn't learnt his spellings and he knew his teacher, Mr Tuck, could get very cross about silly spelling tests.

7

Arthur felt a tug on his hood.

"Guess who I saw on Saturday?" said Gwen, a ten-out-of-ten show-off from Arthur's class. "Robin Bobblecap and his Merry Men."

"You never," said Arthur.

I did! I did! They were chasing the sheriff's soldiers out of Snarewood Forest. Robin gave me a big kiss.

9

Arthur had heard many exciting
stories about the famous outlaws.

"You've given me a great idea," he
said. "I'm going to run away and
become an outlaw."

Arthur tried to run to the school
gates but Gwen hung on to his hood.

"Don't be silly," she said. "You can't
be an outlaw."

Arthur shook himself free.
"Goodbye, Gwen. I'm off to
Snarewood Forest to join Robin
Bobblecap and his Merry Men."

Arthur thought about giving her
a big kiss before he dashed away.
Like a brave outlaw would...

Yuk! He couldn't do it.

He turned and ran straight into
the enormous tummy of his teacher,
Mr Tuck.

"Going somewhere?" asked Mr Tuck
with a wicked smile.

"Snarewood Forest!" shouted Arthur, dodging past his teacher. "I'd rather be an outlaw than do your silly spelling test!"

Mr Tuck and Gwen watched Arthur run away over the fields.

CHAPTER TWO
Arthur's Outlaws

Arthur stood at the edge of Snarewood
Forest and shivered. He peered in at
the shadows under the trees. Everyone
was afraid of Snarewood. Except the
outlaws of course. Slowly he edged his
way amongst the giant trees.

It was horribly quiet and creepy in the great forest. Arthur didn't like it at all.

He would have gone back to school if he hadn't heard the sound of someone pretending to be a horse.

"Ow!" whispered Arthur, whipping his hand off a stinging nettle. Sneaking through forests was not easy to do.

16

He could see the famous Robin Bobblecap skipping about in a clearing, slapping his bottom and occasionally calling out a loud "NNHAAAAAAAAAY!" Watching closely was another famous outlaw – Little Tom, the hairiest of Robin's Merry Men.

Arthur was scared. Everyone knew that outlaws were dangerous. What if they shot him full of arrows as soon as they saw him?

He took a deep breath, raised his hands above his head and stepped out of his hiding place. To his surprise the outlaws didn't notice him.

Then, Little Tom, you throw off your horse disguise, knock down all the guards, break open the castle gates and give three long whistles. That's when I come riding in and rescue Lady Carryon.

"I dunno, Robin... sounds awful tricky," said Little Tom.

Arthur shuffled closer and tried coughing loudly. Still the outlaws ignored him. "What could be tricky about such a simple plan?" said Robin. "Is it the disguise? You make a very good horse, you know."

"No, no… it's not the horse bit," answered Little Tom.

Arthur waved his arms and called, "Excuse me! Mr Bobblecap, sir!"

"Is it the guards? You're not afraid of a few guards are you?" said Robin.

"No, no, of course not," said Little Tom.

Arthur was desperate, he decided to use the ear-splitting bellow he normally saved for his mother.

With a squeal of fright Robin dived behind a fallen tree. Arthur and Little Tom looked at each other for a few moments.

"It's just a little boy, Robin," said Little Tom.

"A little boy? Are you sure?"

Robin Bobblecap peered over the tree and stared fiercely at Arthur.

"You took a risk, boy. Don't you know it's dangerous to sneak up on outlaws? What's your name?"

"Sir... Arthur... sir," gabbled Arthur, trying to be polite.

"Well, Sir Arthur, what are you doing in my forest?" asked Robin.

"I want to be an outlaw," said Arthur.

"Oh you do, do you?" said Robin. "Well, let me tell you this, Sir Arthur, it's not easy being an outlaw."

"No, no... it's awful tricky," said Little Tom.

"I can be an outlaw. Give me a chance, please, sir," said Arthur.

"Outlaws have to be brave and strong!" said Robin. "Outlaws have to be clever and cunning! Outlaws have to be..."

"Able to sneak up on two men and scare the life out of them?" suggested Little Tom.

"Ah yes, indeed," said Robin.

CHAPTER THREE
Arthur's Arrow

"Let's give you a test," said Robin, with a wicked smile that reminded Arthur of his teacher. "Little Tom, my bow!" Robin strode out to the centre of the clearing, hitched up his tights and adjusted his bobblecap. "Fetch this arrow, Sir Arthur, and then we'll see about you becoming an outlaw!"

Little Tom hurried over to Robin carrying a huge longbow. "Sorry, Robin," he muttered, "I can't find yours so you'll have to borrow mine."

"What! This is no good! I can't—" said Robin, stopping short when he saw Arthur watching him.

The bow was bigger than Robin and he struggled and sweated as he pulled back the string. "Fetch this arrow…" he said again, through gritted teeth.

TWANG!

The bow jerked, Robin jumped and the arrow fell at his feet.

Arthur ran forward eagerly. "Not *that* arrow!" snapped Robin. He threw down the bow.

"Little Tom, help me out, will you?"

Little Tom picked up the bow and notched the arrow on the string. Easily he drew the arrow back.

"Fetch *that* arrow," said Robin, pointing. Little Tom fired and the arrow sped away over the trees. Arthur dashed after it.

"That's got rid of him," said Robin. "Now, where were we?"

"It's the bit about whistlin' three times," said Little Tom. "Awful tricky."

Arthur found it very hard to run through the forest while looking up at the sky. Brambles scratched him.

Tree roots tripped him.

Branches whipped him.

And a ditch swallowed him. It was muddy and smelly.

"Little Tom was right," he thought, "it's awful tricky being an outlaw."

Bravely Arthur climbed out of the ditch and continued in the direction of the arrow.

He came to the edge of a river. It looked deep and cold. The arrow had come down on the far side. Arthur needed a plan. How could he cross the river without getting his clothes wet?

He had an idea.
It was very daring.
A real outlaw plan.
He was glad there
was nobody around
to see it, though.
First he took off
all his clothes and
bundled them
together. Then he
paddled into the river.

The water was ice
cold. It rose up past
his knees and up and
up to his tummy. He
kept going and it rose
up to his armpits.

He held his clothes
high above his
head and his teeth
chattered.

Suddenly he slipped and fell. He threw his clothes in the air in a mad attempt to keep them dry and disappeared under the water. He surfaced, gasping and splashing, to see his clothes swirling away downstream.

With a yell he dived after them, caught something and struggled out on to the riverbank. He had saved his vest – a very long, very wet vest.

Arthur felt like crying. But outlaws don't cry. He was determined to find that arrow and take it back to Robin Bobblecap.

Bravely Arthur set off down a path into the forest, his vest dripping around his knees. He had not gone far when he heard the snorting and crashing of some fearful monster coming straight towards him.

Arthur scrambled up the nearest tree
as a huge stag burst on to the path. Its
nostrils snorted angrily and its bulging
eyes stared left and right. It carried a
magnificent set of antlers spoiled only
by an arrow sticking out at a jaunty
angle. It was Robin's arrow!

The stag paused for some extra loud snorts beneath Arthur's tree. Arthur did not wait. His hand shot down and grabbed the arrow. The stag felt the tug and gave a great jerk of its head. Arthur was pulled clean out of the tree on to the deer's back.

With a great bellow the stag charged
off and Arthur hung on for dear life!

Chapter Four
Arthur's Return

In a clearing of Snarewood Forest, Robin Bobblecap was teaching Little Tom how to whistle. "Try to make the hole smaller..."

"Oh, *corsets*, Robin!" snapped Little Tom. "Can't I just do three owl hoots instead?"

Suddenly a great stag bounded into
the clearing with a familiar-looking
boy riding on its back. Snorting and
bellowing, it charged at the two men.

"Run!" shouted Arthur.

They ran.

Robin, never short of a good plan, shouted to Little Tom, "Split up. It will confuse the stag and we might escape! You turn left and I'll turn right! Go!"

Both men turned a sharp right and the stag skidded around after them.

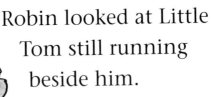

Robin looked at Little
Tom still running
beside him.
"What are you
doing?" he yelled.
"Sorry, Robin. I
never could remember
my left from my right..."
The deer caught them and tossed
them heavily into a thick holly bush.

Arthur had fallen off. The arrow was gone from its antlers. The stag was satisfied so it stalked away back into the trees.

Arthur had been thrown off when the stag had made that sudden right turn. He was delighted to find that he was still holding the arrow. He ran over to the two outlaws who were climbing painfully out of the holly bush.

Robin did not look impressed. He looked prickly.

"You nearly get me killed and then you want to join my outlaws?" he snapped. "Where are your clothes?"

Arthur was embarrassed. "I lost them in the river."

"Outlaws don't *lose* things! They *steal* things," said Robin. "I don't think you're ready yet. I think you need to fetch another arrow. Little Tom, fetch my bow!"

This was too much for Arthur. He felt as mad as a stag. As Robin turned to get his bobblecap out of the holly bush, Arthur jabbed the arrow into the outlaw's bottom. With a terrific yell, Robin dived back into the prickles.

EEEEYOW!!

"Forget it!" shouted Arthur. "I'd rather go back to school than do your silly outlaw test. And I'm *stealing* this!" He snatched up Robin's cloak of green and marched away.

45

> I must not run away from school.
> I must not run away from school.

Back at school, Arthur stopped writing and stretched his aching fingers. Sixty-seven lines written. Thirty-three to go.

He ran his hand over Robin's cloak of green. He couldn't wait to tell Gwen where he'd got it.

The End

Look out for these other titles in the Shooting Stars range:

Cinderella's Wedding by Paeony Lewis
Cinderella loves the Prince and the Prince loves her.
Planning a wedding should be easy... but not if
Cinderella's ugly sisters, Hiccup and Nosy, have
anything to do with it.

My Dad Is... by Ali Ives
When Becky Harris has to write an essay about her dad,
she has a huge problem. She has a wonderful mum, but
she doesn't have a dad! So she decides to make one up.
But none of the dads she invents seems to be quite right.

You can buy all these books from your local bookseller,
or order them direct from the publisher. For more
information about Shooting Stars, write to: *The Sales
Department, Hodder Children's Books, a division of Hodder
Headline, 338 Euston Road, London NW1 3BH.*